AF560647

Quills

Quills

The Hungry Little Porcupine

Shibani Alter

Illustrations by

Shruti Hemani

ALEPH

ALEPH BOOK COMPANY
An independent publishing firm
promoted by ***Rupa Publications India***

First published in India in 2024
by Aleph Book Company
7/16 Ansari Road, Daryaganj
New Delhi 110 002

This is a work of fiction. Names, characters, places, and incidents are either the product of the author's imagination or are used fictitiously and any resemblance to any actual persons, living or dead, events, or locales is entirely coincidental.

ISBN: 978-81-974969-6-7

1 3 5 7 9 10 8 6 4 2

Printed in India

For Dad

Quills

The sun began to set behind the foothills to the west. The orange light retreated across a low ridge and fell into the mouth of a small tunnel at the far end of the mountain. Here, the light stretched and faded into the depths of a muddy burrow. And there, at the end of the dark tunnel, lived a little porcupine named Quills.

Quills opened his eyes after a long day's sleep. He yawned and stretched his little legs. Suddenly, he heard a low growl. Quills leapt out of bed. He looked around the room. There was nobody there. He heard the growl again. He realized the sound was coming from his tummy.

'Oh shucks, tummy, you scared the quills out of me!' said the little porcupine, rubbing his empty belly.

Quills was hungry. So, he wandered into the kitchen to find something to eat. He opened the cupboard doors and scanned the shelves. But all he could find was a shrivelled up old turnip.

'This just won't do,' he sighed and closed the cupboard doors.

Rattling his quills in irritation and twitching his whiskers, he crawled out

of his burrow. Quills stood on the grassy ridge and looked out at the snowy peaks in the distance. The twilight was fading and a new moon was in the sky. As everyone's day was coming to an end, his was just getting started. Quills set his nose to the ground and off he went, in search of something yummy to eat. He made his way down the steep mountain ridge. He padded through a thicket of ferns, wet from the day's rain. He turned left at a field of pink thunder lilies that waved in the gentle breeze. He passed through the forest of rhododendrons where a whistling thrush watched from a branch. He disappeared in the tall grass as he wandered down the overgrown trail.

He crossed the ravine full of boulders covered with moss. He continued beyond the fallen oak that was rotting into the ground.

He scurried along until he came upon a spring. Here, the cold mountain water pooled before it trickled down to the valley. Feeling thirsty after his long walk, Quills eagerly lapped up mouthfuls of fresh spring water.

And that's when he heard a sound in the bushes behind him. Startled, Quills made a run for it as a wild boar came charging through the brush.

'Wait up, Quills!' said the pig as she chased after him.

'Oh shucks, Pig! You scared the quills out of me!' cried the little porcupine.

Pig chuckled. 'I'm not that scary, am I?' Her black wiry hair stood on end, forming a mohawk down her spine, and her little tail looked like a muddy twig.

'No, no. I thought you might be, you-know-who…' said Quills, lowering his voice. Pig leaned in close so Quills could whisper in her ear, 'Leopard.'

Pig shivered with fright. 'Shhh! Don't say such a thing! It's just me!'

And the two friends glanced around to make sure they were alone.

'What are you doing on this side of the hill?' Pig asked Quills.

'I'm looking for something yummy to eat,' said Quills.

'Say no more, I know just the thing,' Pig grinned. And Quills could see that Pig's mouth was already watering.

Pig led Quills to a clearing in the forest. Here, the lush hillside sloped in all directions and fireflies drifted over a field of wildflowers. Pig sniffed and snorted as she ran her nose through the dirt. Quills followed close behind.

'Over here!' called Pig as she began to dig.

So, Quills started to dig too. As they flung the dirt aside, they revealed a tangle of thick white tubers growing underground. Their eyes lit up at the feast before them. They were about to sink their hungry teeth into the fleshy roots, when they heard a sound in the trees above.

Startled, Quills and Pig made a run for it as a monkey came swinging down towards them.

'Wait up, Quills! Wait up, Pig!' said the monkey as he chased after them.

'Oh shucks, Monkey! You scared the quills out of me!' cried the little porcupine.

Monkey chuckled. 'I'm not that scary, am I?' His big eyes peered out from under a fringe of silver hair. His long tail formed a question mark behind him.

'No, no. We thought you might be, you-know-who…' said Pig, lowering her

voice. Monkey leaned in close so Pig could whisper in his ear, 'Leopard.'

Monkey shivered with fright. 'Shhh! Don't say such a thing! It's just me!'

And the three friends glanced around to make sure they were alone.

'What are you doing on this side of the hill?' asked Monkey.

'We were looking for something yummy to eat,' said Quills.

'Say no more, I know just the thing,' Monkey grinned. And Quills and Pig could see that Monkey's mouth was already watering.

Monkey led his friends to a vast orchard. Here, endless rows of trees spread across the mountaintop and the wind rushed through the thick canopy of leaves. Monkey quickly scaled the trunk of a tree and leapt from one branch to another. Quills and Pig followed below.

'Over here!' called Monkey as he shook the branches and one by one, the loquats started to fall.

Quills and Pig gathered them as they fell to the ground. Their eyes lit up at the feast before them. They were about to sink their hungry teeth into the tart fruit, when they heard a sound in the dry leaves nearby.

Startled, Quills, Pig, and Monkey made a run for it as a mongoose came scurrying towards them.

'Wait up, Quills! Wait up, Pig! Wait up, Monkey!' said the mongoose as she

chased after them.

'Oh shucks, Mongoose! You scared the quills out of me!' cried the little porcupine.

Mongoose chuckled. 'I'm not that scary, am I?'

Her pink nose twitched from side to side. She was blanketed in soft grey fur that extended into a bushy tail.

'No, no. We thought you might be, you-know-who…' said Monkey, lowering his voice. Mongoose leaned in close so Monkey could whisper in her ear, 'Leopard.'

Mongoose shivered with fright. 'Shhh! Don't say such a thing! It's just me!'

And the four friends glanced around to make sure they were alone.

'What are you doing on this side of the hill?' asked Mongoose.

'We were looking for something yummy to eat,' said Quills.

'Say no more, I know just the thing,' Mongoose grinned. And Quills, Pig, and Monkey could see that Mongoose's mouth was already watering.

Mongoose led her friends to a moss forest at the far end of the mountain. Here, the thick moss grew over the rocks and coated the trees. Mongoose padded across the soft green carpet, clearing clumps of rot and overturning rocks. Quills, Pig, and Monkey followed close behind.

'Over here!' called Mongoose as she

breathed in the warm musty aroma.

There in front of them was a row of cream-colored mushrooms. Their eyes lit up at the feast before them. They were about to sink their hungry teeth into the soft fungus, when they heard a sound on the rocks nearby.

Startled, Quills, Pig, Monkey, and Mongoose made a run for it as a goat sprung up the rocks and trotted towards them.

'Wait up, Quills! Wait up, Pig! Wait up Monkey! Wait up Mongoose!' said the goat as he chased after them.

'Oh shucks, Goat! You scared the quills out of me!' cried the little porcupine.

Goat chuckled. 'I'm not that scary, am I?' Two spiral horns protruded from his forehead and a shaggy beard hung from his chin.

'No, no. We thought you might be, you-know-who…' said Mongoose, lowering her voice. Goat leaned in close so Mongoose could whisper in his ear, 'Leopard.'

Goat shivered with fright. 'Shhh! Don't say such a thing! It's just me!'

And the five friends glanced around to make sure they were alone.

'What are you doing on this side of the hill?' asked Goat.

'We were looking for something yummy to eat,' said Quills.

‘Say no more, I know just the thing,’ Goat grinned. And Quills, Pig, Monkey, and Mongoose could see that Goat’s mouth was already watering.

Goat led his friends to a rocky outcropping. Here, a series of rock formations surrounded a hidden clover field. Goat bounded over the rocks and waded through the green field. Quills, Pig, Monkey, and Mongoose followed close behind.

‘Over here!’ called Goat as he ran his snout through the clover.

There, hidden amongst the weeds was a cluster of wild strawberries. Their eyes lit up at the feast before them. They were about to sink their hungry teeth into the sweet fruit, when they heard a low growl.

Startled, Pig disappeared into the brush. Monkey leapt into a nearby tree. Mongoose took cover under the leaves. Goat hid behind the rocks.

But Quills didn't move. He looked down at his belly. 'Yes, yes tummy, I know you're hungry and we're finally going to eat,' Quills said to himself. And then the growl grew louder.

'Hi there, Quills,' said a menacing voice.

The little porcupine felt a hot breath float over him and settle along his quills. He turned and came face to face with Leopard who had been hiding in the tall grass. His quills rattled with fright; his

whiskers twitched with all their might.

'I'm not that scary, am I?' Leopard said knowingly.

Her sleek powerful body loomed over Quills. Her spots shone in the evening light.

Quills swallowed hard, too afraid to speak.

'You're right, I am scary,' said Leopard, smirking wickedly. 'What are you doing on this side of the hill?' asked Leopard.

'We were looking for something yummy to eat,' whispered Quills.

'You don't say? So am I.'

And Quills could see that Leopard's mouth was already watering.

‘And it looks like I found it,’ Leopard purred.

That’s when Leopard opened her mouth, let out a loud roar, and lunged at

Quills. But soon that mighty roar turned into a scared, painful whimper.

'Oh shucks, Leopard! You scared the quills out of me!' cried the little porcupine.

Quills looked at Leopard apologetically.

Leopard backed away slowly, whimpering and pawing at the sharp quills jutting out of her snout. Pig peeked out from the brush. Monkey looked down from the tree. Mongoose peered out from under the leaves. Goat watched from behind the rocks.

'Run for it, Quills!' they shouted.

So Quills ran as fast as his little legs could carry him. Beyond the fallen oak. Across the ravine. Into the tall grass. Through the forest of rhododendrons.

Right at the field of pink thunder lilies. Over the thicket of ferns, Along the steep grassy ridge. To the mouth of his burrow. Quills dove in and wiggled and wriggled his way down the tunnel as fast as he could, until he was finally home; safe and sound.

Quills climbed into bed. He was still shaking with fright. His quills rattled and his whiskers twitched. He pulled the covers over his head.

And that's when he heard the sound he had been dreading. It was a low growl. Quills leapt out of bed. He looked around the room. There was nobody there. He heard the growl again. It was his tummy.

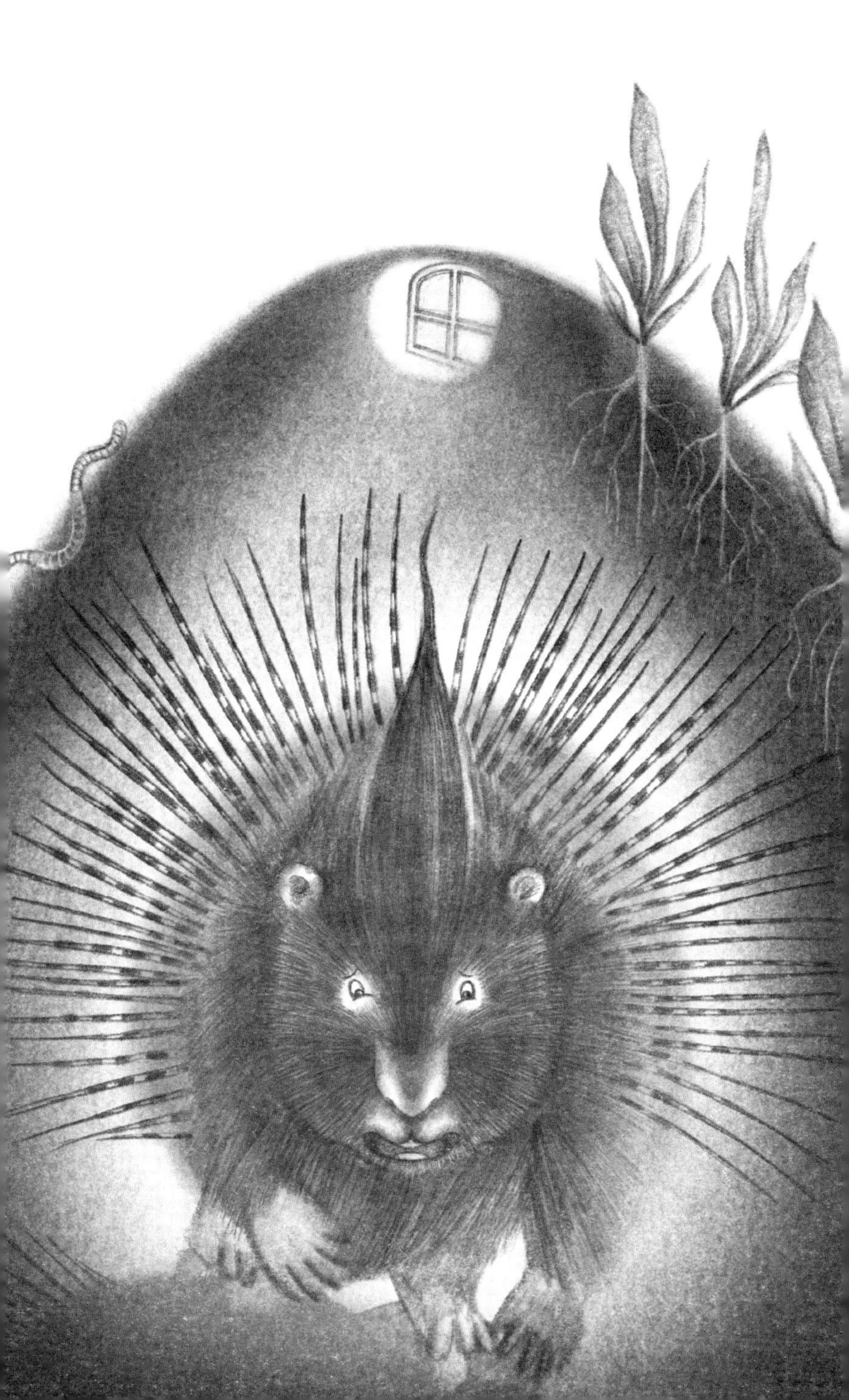

'Oh shucks, tummy, you scared the quills out of me!' said the little porcupine, rubbing his empty belly.

Quills wandered into the kitchen. He opened the cupboard doors and scanned the shelves. He found the shrivelled up old turnip and turned it over in his hands.

'I guess this will have to do,' said Quills, closing the cupboard doors.

He was too afraid to go outside. So, he brought the wrinkled vegetable to his mouth. He was about to sink his hungry teeth into the wilted turnip, when he heard a sound coming from beyond his burrow.

'Quills!' Someone was calling his name.

Quills listened carefully. 'Who's there?' he called out.

'Quills, it's us!' said the familiar voices.

Quills cautiously crawled through his tunnel and peered out from his muddy burrow. There before him were his friends, Pig, Monkey, Mongoose, and Goat.

Pig had brought as many tubers as he could dig up from the ground. Monkey had brought as many loquats as he could shake from the trees. Mongoose had brought as many mushrooms as he could find under the rocks. Goat had brought as many wild strawberries as he could pluck from the clover.

'We brought you some yummy things

to eat,' said the friends in unison.

Quills looked at the shrivelled up old turnip in his hands and then smiled at his friends.

The five friends stood along the grassy ridge. Their eyes lit up and their mouths watered as they sunk their hungry teeth into the much deserved feast. They heard a rustling sound from above. An owl called out from the trees overhead. But none of the friends made a move. They had nothing to fear. Leopard was miles away and nursing a sore snout. So Quills, Pig, Monkey, Mongoose, and Goat ate until their bellies were full. They talked until there was nothing left to say. And then they curled up in the grass

and closed their eyes. The sun began to rise. Dawn turned to day. The light blanketed the friends. And their gentle snores drifted out into the mountain air.